Dear Parent:

Congratulations! Your child is taking the first steps on an exciting journey. The destination? Independent reading!

STEP INTO READING® will help your child get there. The program offers five steps to reading success. Each step includes fun stories and colorful art. There are also Step into Reading Sticker Books, Step into Reading Math Readers, Step into Reading Phonics Readers, Step into Reading Write-In Readers, and Step into Reading Phonics Boxed Sets—a complete literacy program with something to interest every child.

Learning to Read, Step by Step!

Ready to Read Preschool–Kindergarten
• big type and easy words • rhyme and rhythm • picture clues
For children who know the alphabet and are eager to begin reading.

Reading with Help Preschool–Grade 1
• basic vocabulary • short sentences • simple stories
For children who recognize familiar words and sound out new words with help.

Reading on Your Own Grades 1–3
• engaging characters • easy-to-follow plots • popular topics
For children who are ready to read on their own.

Reading Paragraphs Grades 2–3
• challenging vocabulary • short paragraphs • exciting stories
For newly independent readers who read simple sentences with confidence.

Ready for Chapters Grades 2–4
• chapters • longer paragraphs • full-color art
For children who want to take the plunge into chapter books but still like colorful pictures.

STEP INTO READING® is designed to give every child a successful reading experience. The grade levels are only guides. Children can progress through the steps at their own speed, developing confidence in their reading, no matter what their grade.

Remember, a lifetime love of reading starts with a single step!

For Ruby, Lucas,
and Theo
—J.L.

Copyright © 2016 Disney Enterprises, Inc. All rights reserved. The movie THE PRINCESS AND THE FROG Copyright © 2009 Disney, story inspired in part by the book THE FROG PRINCESS by E.D. Baker Copyright © 2002, published by Bloomsbury Publishing, Inc. Published in the United States by Random House Children's Books, a division of Penguin Random House LLC, 1745 Broadway, New York, NY 10019, and in Canada by Penguin Random House Canada Limited, Toronto, in conjunction with Disney Enterprises, Inc.

Step into Reading, Random House, and the Random House colophon are registered trademarks of Penguin Random House LLC.

Visit us on the Web!
StepIntoReading.com
randomhousekids.com

Educators and librarians, for a variety of teaching tools, visit us at
RHTeachersLibrarians.com

ISBN 978-0-7364-3664-9 (trade) — ISBN 978-0-7364-8191-5 (lib. bdg.)
ISBN 978-0-7364-3665-6 (ebook)

Printed in the United States of America   10 9 8 7 6 5 4 3

DISNEY
PRINCESS

Happy Birthday, Princess!

by Jennifer Liberts
illustrated by Elisa Marrucchi

Random House 🏠 New York

Belle's birthday party
is so much fun!

Belle shares cake
with everyone.

Gifts for Tiana.

Lights that glow.

Cinderella's gifts have lots of bows.

A wish come true!
Golden lights.

Birthday candles
shining bright!

Balloons
for Snow White.
Friends who care.

Jasmine has lots
of goodies to share!

Play a game.

Have some fun!

Cupcakes
for Ariel!
Yum, yum, yum!

Happy birthday,
Princess!